You have heard of Mother Goose.
But who is Mother Goose?
Is she a real goose wearing a little white hat,
as she is in France?

Is she an old countrywoman with a tall hat
and a shawl, as she is in England?

Or is she Elizabeth Foster,
who lived on Pudding Lane
and married Isaac Goose of Boston?

Abbott

Chadwick

Wadsworth

Tawny

Stuart

Nickleby

Baxter

Elizabeth Foster

Elizabeth Foster was a young woman
from the country. In 1692, she married
old Isaac Goose from the city, a widower
with ten children.
Together they had four more.
Elizabeth Goose was certainly a mother,
and she also was a Goose.

Filmore

Fern

Hazel

Hadley

Dita

Isaac Goose

Elizabeth

Rutherford

She must have told stories.
She probably recited rhymes.
With fourteen children, how could she
not sing lullabies?
Here is the story of Mother Goose
of Pudding Lane. Now you can decide
who is the real Mother Goose.

MOTHER GOOSE

told by CHRIS RASCHKA

 Candlewick Press
99 Dover Street, Somerville,
MA 09144

Of PUDDING LANE

PicTuRes By VLaDIMiR RaDunsky

 First edition 2019. Library of Congress Catalog Card Number pending. ISBN 978-0-7636-7523-3. This book was typeset in HH Firmin Didot and JacobRiley. The illustrations were done in gouache and pencil. Candlewick Press, 99 Dover Street, Somerville, Massachusetts 02144. visit us at www.candlewick.com. Printed in Shenzhen, Guangdong, China. 19 20 21 22 23 24 CCP 10 9 8 7 6 5 4 3 2 1

Elizabeth Goose
Met
Isaac Goose,
Who loved her from the start.

As I was going up Pippen Hill,
Pippen Hill was dirty.
There I met a pretty miss
And she dropt me a curtsy.
Little miss, pretty miss,
Blessings light upon you!
If I had half a crown a day,
I'd spend it gladly on you.

Mirror, mirror, tell me,
Am I pretty or plain?
Or am I downright ugly
And ugly to remain?
Shall I marry a gentleman?
Shall I marry a clown?
Or shall I marry old Knives-and-Scissors
Shouting through the town?

Elizabeth Goose
Asked
Isaac Goose,
"Will you be my true heart?"

On Saturday night
shall be my care
To powder my locks
and curl my hair.

On Sunday morning
my love will come in,
When he will marry me
with a gold ring.

Elizabeth Goose
With
Isaac Goose
Began her life anew.

Lavender blue and rosemary green,
When I am king you shall be queen;
Call up my maids at four o'clock,
Some to the wheel and some to the rock;
Some to make hay and some to shear corn,
And you and I will keep the bed warm.

In a cottage in Fife

Lived a man with his wife,
Who, believe me, were comical folk:
For, to people's surprise,
They both saw with their eyes,
And their tongues moved whenever they spoke!
When quite fast asleep,
I've been told that to keep
Their eyes open they could not contrive;
They walked on their feet,
It was thought what they eat
Helped, with drinking, to keep them alive!
What's amazing to tell,
I have heard that their smell
Chiefly lay in a thing called their nose!
And though strange are such tales,
On their fingers they'd nails,
As well as on each of their toes!

January

Married when the year is new,
He'll be loving, kind, and true.

February

When February birds do mate,
You either wed or dread your fate.

May

Marry in the month of May,
And you'll surely rue the day.

June

Marry when June roses grow,
Over land and sea you'll go.

September

Marry in September's shine,
Your living will be rich and fine.

October

If in October you do marry,
Love will come, but riches tarry.

March

If you wed when March winds blow,
Joy and sorrow you'll both know.

April

Marry in April when you can,
Joy for maiden and for man.

July

Those who in July are wed
Must labor for their daily bread.

August

Whoever wed in August be,
Many a change is sure to see.

November

If you wed in bleak November,
Only joys will come, remember.

December

When December snows fall fast,
Marry, and true love will last.

Elizabeth Goose
And
Isaac Goose
Had children quite a few.

There was an old woman who lived in a shoe,
She had so many children,
She didn't know what to do,
She gave them some broth without any bread;
She whipped them all soundly and put them to bed.

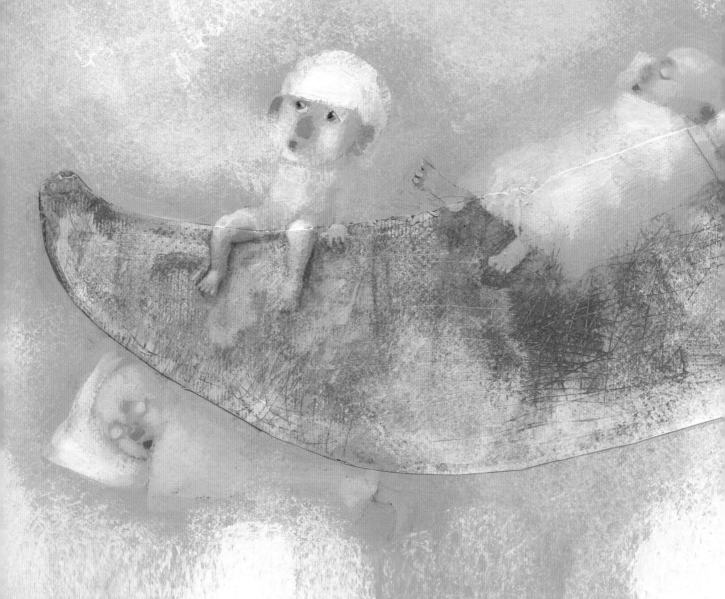

Elizabeth Goose
With
Isaac Goose
Did raise a family.

Diddle, diddle, dumpling, my son John,
Went to bed with his trousers on;
One shoe off, and one shoe on,
Diddle, diddle, dumpling, my son John.

There was a little green house, and in the little green house there was a little white house, and in the little white house there was a little brown house, and in the little brown house there was a little yellow house, and in the little yellow house there was a little heart!

All work and no play
makes Jack a **dull boy;**

All play and no work

makes Jack a **mere toy.**

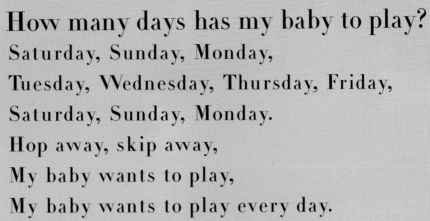

How many days has my baby to play?
Saturday, Sunday, Monday,
Tuesday, Wednesday, Thursday, Friday,
Saturday, Sunday, Monday.
Hop away, skip away,
My baby wants to play,
My baby wants to play every day.

Elizabeth Goose
That
Family Goose
Now filled with poetry.

Old King Cole

Was a merry old soul,
And a merry old soul was he;
He called for his pipe,
And he called for his bowl,
And he called for his fiddlers three.

Every fiddler, he had a fiddle,
And a very fine fiddle had he;
Twee tweedle dee, tweedle dee, went the fiddlers.
Oh, there's none so rare
As can compare
With King Cole and his fiddlers three.

Baa, baa, black sheep,
Have you any wool?
Yes, sir, yes, sir,
Three bags full,
One for the master,
One for the dame,
One for the little boy
Who lives in the lane.

Hush, little baby, don't say a word,
Papa's going to buy you a mockingbird.

If the mockingbird don't sing,
Papa's going to buy you a diamond ring.

If the diamond ring turns to brass,
Papa's going to buy you a looking glass.

If the looking glass gets broke,
Papa's going to buy you a billy goat.

If the billy goat runs away,
Papa's going to buy you another today.

Elizabeth Goose
The
Family Goose
Did counsel and advise.

The cock crows in the morn
To tell us to rise,
And he that lies late
Will never be wise:

For early to bed
And early to rise
Is the way to be healthy
And wealthy and wise.

Go to bed late,

Stay very small;

Go to bed early,

Grow very tall.

Elizabeth Goose
To the
Family Goose
Was motherly and wise.

Little Miss Lily,
You're dreadfully silly
To wear such a very long skirt.
If you take my advice,
You would hold it up nice
And not let it trail in the dirt.

Goosey, goosey gander,
Whither shall I wander?
Upstairs and downstairs
And in my lady's chamber.
There I met an old man
Who would not say his prayers.
I took him by the left leg
And threw him down the stairs.

Gregory Griggs, Gregory Griggs,

Had twenty-seven different wigs.

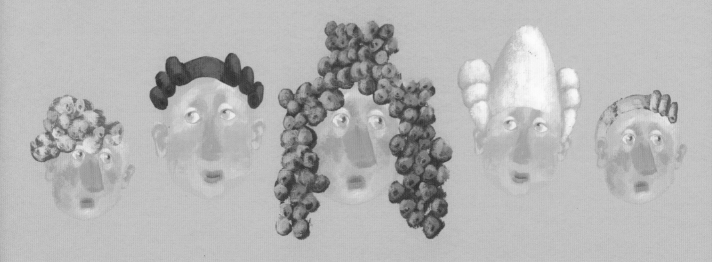

He wore them up, he wore them down,

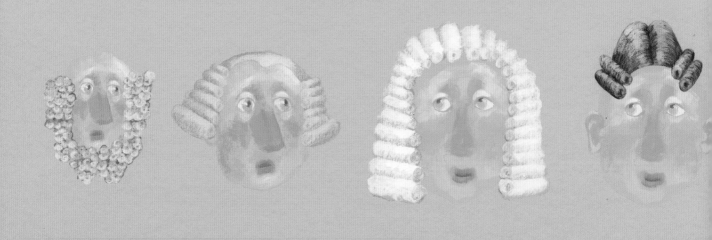

To please the people of the town.

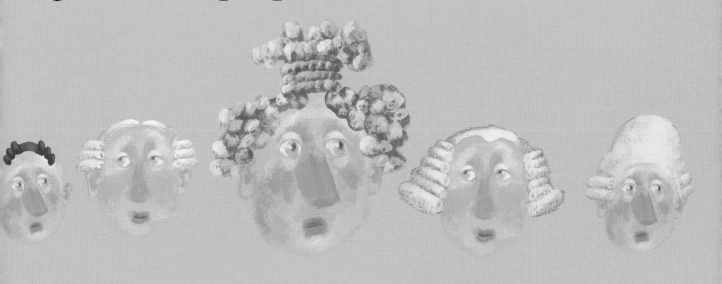

He wore them east, he wore them west,

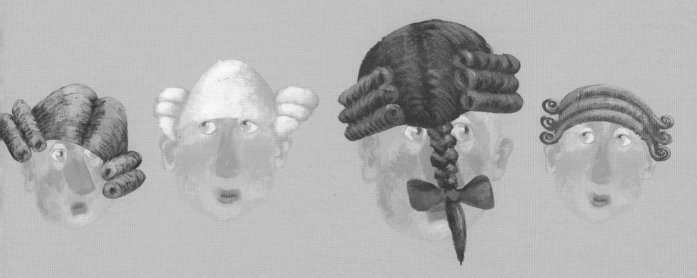

And never could tell which one he liked best.

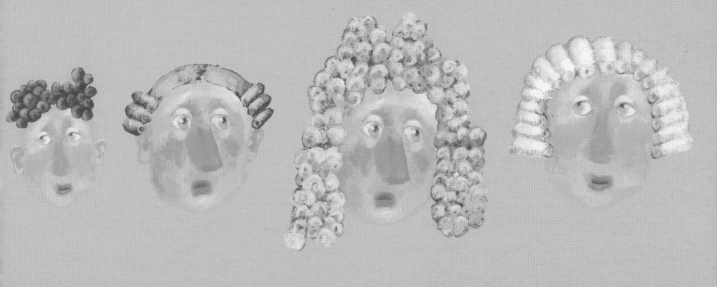

The Family Goose,
Thought
Elizabeth Goose,
Was sometimes like a zoo.

Oh where, oh where has my little dog gone?
Oh where, oh where can he be?
With his ears cut short and his tail cut long,
Oh where, oh where is he?

Chook, chook, chook, chook, chook,
Good morning, Mrs. Hen.
How many chickens have you got?
Madam, I've got ten.
Four of them are yellow,
And four of them are brown,
And two of them are speckled red,
The nicest in the town.

"Elizabeth Goose,"
Quipped
Isaac Goose,
"A poetess are you."

Barber, barber, shave a pig,
How many hairs to make a wig?
Four and twenty, that's enough,
Give the barber a pinch of snuff.

A little pig found a fifty-dollar note
And purchased a hat and a very fine coat,
With trousers, and stockings, and shoes,
Cravat, and shirt-collar, and gold-headed cane,
Then proud as could be, did he march up the lane;
Says he, "I shall hear all the news."

Elizabeth Goose
Loved
Isaac Goose
Through summer, spring, and fall.

If you sneeze on Monday, you sneeze for danger;

Sneeze on a Tuesday, kiss a stranger;

Sneeze on a Wednesday, sneeze for a letter;

Sneeze on a Thursday, **something better**;

Sneeze on a Friday, sneeze for **sorrow**;

Sneeze on a Saturday, **joy tomorrow.**

Ahchoo!

"Elizabeth Goose,"
Said
Isaac Goose,
"I love you best of all."

Curly locks, Curly locks,
Wilt thou be mine?
Thou shalt not wash dishes
Nor yet feed the swine,
But sit on a cushion
And sew a fine seam,
And feed upon strawberries,
Sugar, and cream.

Roses are **red,**

Violets are **blue,**

Sugar is **sweet**

And so are **you.**

Elizabeth Goose
And
Isaac Goose
At last grew old and gray.

Old woman, old woman, shall we go a-shearing?
Speak a little louder, sir, I'm very thick of hearing.
Old woman, old woman, shall we go a-gleaning?
Speak a little louder, sir, I cannot tell your meaning.
Old woman, old woman, shall we go a-walking?
Speak a little louder, sir, or what's the use of talking?
Old woman, old woman, shall I kiss you dearly?
Thank you, kind sir, I hear you very clearly.

Elizabeth Goose,
As
Mother Goose,
Can still be heard today.

Good night, sleep tight,
Don't let the bedbugs bite.

A.B and C.
I'll fight you all Three

D. E. and F,
we'll make him quite deaf.

K.L. and M.
will you fight again

N. O. and P.
shall we go and see.

T. U. and V.
cannot you see .

W. X. Y.
I'll make you to cry